David Dixon's Day as a Dachshund

Follow Your Nose!

CLASS CRITTERS

Book 2

David Dixon's Day as a Dachshund

By Kathryn Holmes
Illustrated by Ariel Landy

AMULET BOOKS • NEW YORK

Follow Your Nose!

Library of Congress Cataloging-in-Publication Data
Names: Holmes, Kathryn, 1982- author. | Landy, Ariel, illustrator.
Title: David Dixon's day as a dachshund / by Kathryn Holmes ; illustrated by Ariel Landy.
Description: New York : Amulet Books, [2022]. | Series: Class critters ; 2 | Audience: Ages 6 to 9. | Summary: When impulsive David brings his new Dachshund puppy, Bandit, into Mrs. Norrell's second-grade class for show-and-tell the dog escapes, and when David rushes off to find him he suddenly turns into a Dachshund himself. Includes "Top ten things about Dachshunds."
Identifiers: LCCN 2021042221 | ISBN 9781419755682 (hardcover) | ISBN 9781647005450 (ebook)
Subjects: LCSH: Dachshunds—Juvenile fiction. | Puppies—Juvenile fiction. | Impulsive personality—Juvenile fiction. | Show-and-tell presentations—Juvenile fiction. | Elementary schools—Juvenile fiction. | CYAC: Dachshunds—Fiction. | Dogs—Fiction. | Impulsive personality—Fiction. | Show-and-tell presentations—Fiction. | Schools—Fiction. | BISAC: JUVENILE FICTION / Readers / Chapter Books | JUVENILE FICTION / Animals / Pets
Classification: LCC PZ7.H7358 Dav 2022 | DDC 813.6 [Fic]—dc23
LC record available at https://lccn.loc.gov/2021042221

ABRAMS The Art of Books
195 Broadway, New York, NY 10007
abramsbooks.com

For Turner,
Benton, and Miles

Best Idea Ever

David Dixon's backpack wouldn't stop wiggling.

As he walked quickly down the hall toward Mrs. Norrell's room, David hugged the backpack tight to his chest. He couldn't wait for show-and-tell time. Judging by the squirms and shimmies coming from his bag, neither could his surprise.

"Almost there," David whispered into the gap he'd left at the top of the zipper so his surprise could breathe.

"Who are you talking to?"

"Nobody!" David yelped, spinning around.

His classmate Riley stared at him, hands on her hips. "What's in your backpack?"

"Nothing."

David's backpack sneezed.

Riley raised her eyebrows.

"Fine," David said. "It's my show-and-tell."

"What is it?"

"It's a secret."

Riley stared him down. "Tell me."

David stared back. "Not yet."

After a long pause—long enough that

David wondered if Riley was going to ruin everything by being a tattletale—she shrugged. "You owe me. Call on me first."

David breathed a sigh of relief. "I will."

He followed Riley into Mrs. Norrell's room. Most days, he was the last kid in his seat. Today, he went to his desk right away, tucking his twitching backpack under his chair.

David sat in the front row. He'd wanted to be in the back next to his best friend, Owen. Unfortunately, their teacher last year, Mrs. Hoang, had warned Mrs. Norrell to separate them. Plus, sitting up front was supposed to help David stay focused.

David had a brain that was full of ideas.

Big, messy, wacky, wonderful ideas.

Like the time he and Owen had found some paint in David's dad's storage shed.

Mrs. Hoang had recently read them a book about the artist Jackson Pollock. David had stared at the colors—fire-truck red, sunshine yellow, robin's-egg blue—and he'd had an idea:

What if they splatter-painted his garage door?

It had been a true masterpiece.

Then there was the first-grade trip to the science museum. David had been learning about how blood moved through the body, and he'd had an idea:

What if he and Owen were blood cells, and the hallways were veins and arteries?

They'd raced around for half an hour before Mrs. Hoang caught up with them.

David's ideas didn't always end in triumph, but sometimes things worked out perfectly. Today was going to be one of those days.

Owen walked in the door. David waved him over and positioned him between the backpack and Mrs. Norrell. "Stand here."

"Okay," Owen said. This was one of the

4

great things about Owen. He always went
along with what David said to do.

"Look." David bent down and unzipped his
bag so Owen could see inside.

Owen's eyes went wide behind his glasses.
"Is that . . . ?"

"It sure is."

"Do your parents know?"

David waved away the question. "I didn't ask them. They would've said no." He quickly put the bag back under his chair. "I have to call on Riley first during show-and-tell. But you'll be second—"

"Everyone, take your seats!" Mrs. Norrell said. When Owen lingered, she added, "You too, Owen."

David didn't want the teacher to think they were up to something . . . even though they kind of were. "Go," he told his best friend. "And don't say a word to anyone!"

"I won't." Owen went to his desk.

When Mrs. Norrell turned around to face the chalkboard, David did an excited wriggle in his chair. Then he leaned down to touch his backpack. The puppy inside nuzzled into his palm.

David had a lot of ideas. He was an idea machine.

This was his best idea ever.

The Opposite of Boring

"Who would like to go first for show-and-tell?" Mrs. Norrell asked when she'd finished making morning announcements.

David's hand shot up like a rocket. "Me!"

Mrs. Norrell nodded. "Okay, David. You're up."

"Yeah!" David jumped out of his seat and pumped his fists. Then he crouched and unzipped his bag. "Hi," he whispered as he reached inside. "All right, I've got you—hey!" he shouted, feeling small, sharp teeth nip at his fingers.

His classmates giggled. Most of them had been in school with David since kindergarten. They knew that whatever was coming would be the opposite of boring.

"David," Mrs. Norrell said, stepping closer. "What—"

"We got a dog this weekend!" David straightened, holding his squirming puppy high. "His name is Bandit. He's a dachshund—a wiener dog. And—ah!"

Bandit launched himself into the air, twisting and flipping like an acrobat.

David dropped to one knee and caught the puppy before he hit the floor.

In the last row, Owen started a round of applause. David stood and took a bow, and then grinned at his best friend. Owen always had his back.

9

Mrs. Norrell didn't seem impressed. "David, I don't think it's a good idea for Bandit to be here."

"Are you kidding?" David looked at the excited puppy. "He loves it!"

"Still, it might not be safe," Mrs. Norrell said. "Do you know how old he is?"

"Eight weeks."

"He's so young. He needs to settle in with your family before he visits a busy place like this school. You have to think about what's best for Bandit—not just what seems fun to you."

David frowned. Mrs. Norrell sounded like his parents. *Taking care of a puppy is a big job*, they'd said. *You need to show us that we can trust you to be responsible for him.*

"Bandit *is* safe here," David told his teacher. "When he jumped, I caught him."

Mrs. Norrell went to the door. "I'll get someone to stay with the class, so you and I can go to the office. We'll call your parents to come get Bandit."

"Wait!" David cried. "Can I at least finish show-and-tell?"

Mrs. Norrell hesitated, her hand on the doorknob.

"I bet everyone has a ton of questions," David said. Sure enough, a bunch of his classmates' hands were raised. Owen had one knee on his seat to lift himself higher. Farrah was waving her arm around like she was trying to say hello to someone really, really far away. Even Victoria looked interested, and she usually acted like she hated everything. "Please," David begged. "Two minutes."

Mrs. Norrell let her hand drop. "Two minutes." She left the door cracked.

David called on Riley first, because he had to.

"Did you get Bandit from a pet store or an animal shelter?" Riley asked.

"Neither! Our two-doors-down neighbors' dog had puppies. Bandit has two brothers

11

and four sisters!" David pointed to his best friend next.

"Did you name him yourself?" Owen asked.

"Yeah. I picked Bandit because this dark part around his eyes looks like a mask."

"Does Bandit get to sleep in your bed?" Farrah shouted, without being called on.

"Farrah," Mrs. Norrell warned gently.

"Not yet," David answered. "He can when he's trained. I don't want him to pee on me in the middle of the night."

The room erupted into squeals and groans.

"All right, one more question," Mrs. Norrell said.

"Aw, come on!" David argued. "No way has it been two minutes!"

His teacher gave him a look.

David sighed. "Who has a really, *really* good question?"

Everyone's voices piled on top of each other: "Me! Me! Pick me!"

David let the moment stretch out. It was fun to be the center of attention. Even if Bandit did have to go home after this, it really had been the best idea—

Bandit sank his pointy teeth into the skin between David's index finger and thumb.

"Argh!" David yelled, yanking his hand away.

Bandit pressed his hind feet into David's chest and pushed off. He landed on the tile floor next to the open door, already running.

Then he was gone.

Thinking Like a Dog

Everyone started talking at once.

"What are we going to—"

"I *knew* this would happen—"

"We have to catch him!"

"I volunteer!"

David ran to the open door. He looked down the hall to the right. He looked down the hall to the left. He looked right again and left again. Bandit was nowhere to be seen.

"Bandit!" he called. "Here, boy!"

Owen appeared beside him, also shouting. "Bandit! Bandit, come back!"

Mrs. Norrell pulled them both away from the doorway. "David, are you bleeding?"

David shook his head. The bite had stung, but Bandit hadn't broken the skin.

His teacher examined his hand. "Maybe you should see the nurse . . ."

"I'm fine," David said quickly. Normally, he would jump at any excuse to visit the nurse's office. Going to the nurse meant getting out of class for a while. The new girl, Tally Tuttle, had gone to the nurse's office on the first day of school and hadn't come back for hours and hours. When David had asked Tally what she'd done in there all day, Tally had drawn her fingers across her mouth, zipping her lips with a secretive smile.

Tally was hiding something . . . something *fun*. David was sure of it.

He would have to solve that mystery another time. Now, he had a puppy to catch.

Mrs. Norrell let go of his hand and stepped away to calm the rest of the class.

David grabbed Owen by the shoulders. "I'm going to find Bandit."

"I'll come with you."

"No. I need you to stay here."

"Why?"

David cut his eyes toward Mrs. Norrell. "I need you to stop her from calling my parents until I'm back."

"Okay, but—"

"They'll be less mad if she calls and I *have* Bandit, than if she calls and I *don't*," David explained. "Make her wait for me. Do whatever it takes."

Owen nodded seriously. "Whatever it takes."

"Thanks." David bolted into the hall, thinking like a dog. *If I were a puppy on the loose in an elementary school, where would I go?*

He started getting ideas.

Big, messy, wacky, wonderful ideas.

Breaking into the art supply closet and turning all of the tissue paper into colorful confetti. Creating an obstacle course in the gymnasium, using rubber balls and jump ropes and hula hoops. Infiltrating the nurse's office

to . . . well, he wasn't sure what he'd do in there, but there had to be *something* a puppy would want to play with or chew on or roll around in.

Plus, in every classroom, there were kids who would love to make friends with a puppy. Imagine all the belly scratches! All the ear rubs! All the snuggles and tickles!

Honestly, being a dog sounded pretty great.

David skidded to a stop at the end of the long hallway. "I wish *I* was a dog," he said.

Cold air slammed into him, like the A/C had just kicked on full blast.

There was a loud sound, like a popping balloon, followed by a tinkly noise that reminded David of the wind chimes his grandma had on her porch.

The air smelled like a wet dog that had been bathed in lemon-lime shampoo.

David felt disoriented. He tried to shake himself out of it. He shook his head, then his shoulders, then his front legs, his tummy, his back legs, his rear end, and finally his tail.

Wait a second.

His tail?!

David twisted in one direction. He saw a tail. He twisted in the other direction. He still saw a tail. Attached to that tail was a long, skinny body covered in black-brown fur.

He yelped. It came out more like a yip.

David Dixon had turned into a dachshund.

4

Rock Star, Race Car

David couldn't believe it. He'd wished to become a dog, and now he was one! This was so cool. He started wagging his tail. The movement felt good—*really* good—like his bones were vibrating with happiness.

He heard a tapping sound behind him. He turned around to see what it was, and it stopped. He turned the other way, and it started up again. What was it? It had a nice beat. It made him want to dance.

Oh! It was his tail, hitting the wall as it wagged! He had his own personal drum kit!

That realization made David's tail move even faster.

He could start a band. An all-dog band! David would be the percussionist. He'd learned about percussion in music class: drums and sticks and maracas and cymbals. But who would be the singer?

Maybe David could sing and play percussion at the same time. It would take practice, but that was fine. His dad liked to say that

anything worth doing was worth doing right. Becoming the world's first canine rock star was absolutely worth doing.

David barked, testing out his voice. The sound was clear and loud and satisfying. What other noises could he make? He yipped and howled. He gruffed and growled.

Bark! Woof! Rowrrr . . . yap! Yip yap! AaaaaOOOOO—

"There he is!" a man shouted from down the hall. It was the janitor. Mr. Bruce was about the same age as David's dad, but he was short and stocky with reddish-brown hair, while David's father was tall and skinny with the same dark hair as David.

There was something David had always wanted to ask Mr. Bruce. "Excuse me. Is Bruce your first name or your last name?" he barked.

The janitor didn't answer. He just kept moving closer.

"Is it *both* your names? Are you Bruce Bruce?"

"That's right," the janitor said.

"Bruce Bruce!" David yapped. "What a great name!"

"Stay there," Mr. Bruce replied. "That's a good dog."

"Oh, I'm not really a dog," David woofed. "I'm David Dixon, from Mrs. Norrell's class. You're probably looking for my puppy, Bandit. Don't worry. I'm going to find him. In fact, you can relax. I've got everything under control."

"Chatty little guy, aren't you?" Mr. Bruce was holding something. It was thin and coiled, with a metal clip on one end.

"What's that?" David tilted his head to get a better look. Now that he thought about it, his vision was kind of blurry. Also, the world was a lot less colorful than it used to be. Everything was blue and yellow and brown and gray. "Is that . . . a leash?"

The janitor crouched in front of him.

David's whole body went tense. "I don't want a leash," he barked, suddenly not sure the janitor could understand him after all.

Mr. Bruce pounced.

David ran.

Running felt *good*. David's toenails clicked against the hard floor. His big ears flapped in the breeze. His tail stuck straight out behind him, making him feel as aerodynamic as a race car zipping around the track.

Rock star, race car . . . David had only been a dog for a few minutes, and already he was achieving some lifelong dreams.

He rounded a corner and darted into the main office. This was where the principal,

Mr. Angelo, hung out with the vice principal and all the other grown-ups who weren't teachers or cafeteria workers or the janitor. David had been here a bunch of times—usually after doing something big, messy, wacky, and wonderful.

Now, he ducked under a desk. A moment later, he heard Mr. Bruce. "He got away from me," the janitor said. "Did you see anything?"

"No dogs in here," said Mrs. Philippidis, the principal's assistant. She had a kind voice and a kind face. Also, she smelled nice, like . . .

David sniffed the air. Sugar cookies and pinecones. Yum. He'd never noticed how good Mrs. Philippidis smelled before.

But her scent wasn't the only one tickling David's nose. There was something else . . . David put his snout to the carpet and breathed in deep. Whatever it was smelled warm and furry and slobbery.

"Psst! Over here!"

David looked, and his eyes went wide.

His missing puppy was staring right at him.

5

So Many Smells to Smell

"Bandit!" David whispered. "I was looking for you!"

"You found me!" the puppy answered from under the next desk. "Now what?"

David had planned to catch Bandit and bring him straight back to Mrs. Norrell's room. He hadn't planned on turning into a dog himself. Nothing like this had ever happened to him before. Why not have a little fun before returning to class?

The ideas he'd had earlier about everything a puppy could get up to in an

elementary school flashed across his mind. If David and Bandit stuck together from now on, that counted as him being responsible for the puppy . . . right?

"We should play chase," Bandit decided.

"I love playing chase," David said eagerly.

"Great! On three," Bandit said. "One . . ."

"I'll keep looking," Mr. Bruce announced. "Call me if you see the dog."

Bandit's tiny bottom twitched with antici-pation. "Two . . ."

Mrs. Philippidis replied to the janitor, "I will."

"Three!" Bandit took off.

David followed him.

The two dogs raced through the office. At first, David stayed right on Bandit's tail. But then Bandit found a ramp: two tote bags with a jacket draped over them, propped against a small lidded wastebasket. The puppy ran up the incline onto a stack of printer paper.

David was bigger than Bandit. When he stepped onto the squishy tote-bag-jacket ramp, it sank beneath his weight. That meant he had to climb onto the paper stack—hard to do, with his short dachshund legs.

By the time David made it up, Bandit was already dashing across the low storage shelf beneath the printer. He was heading for the main office door, which Mr. Bruce had left open just wide enough for a puppy to squeeze through. Bandit took a flying leap and was gone before a single grown-up saw him.

David jumped over to the shelf. He ran across it and tried to dive through the open doorway into the hall after Bandit. Instead of passing cleanly through the slim gap, as Bandit had, David bumped the door, swinging it farther open.

As he ran away, he heard the door slam into the wall. He also heard shouting. Bandit may have made it out unnoticed, but David sure hadn't. And now Bandit had vanished again.

David sniffed the air, searching for that warm, furry, slobbery Bandit-scent. While the transformation had made his eyesight worse, his nose seemed supercharged. It was like swimming in an ocean of odors. There were so many smells to smell!

The crisp printer paper he'd stepped on during his escape a moment ago. The lukewarm coffee in the travel mug on Mrs. Philippidis's desk. Permanent markers and dry-erase markers and Magic Markers in the supply closet. Soaps and shampoos and perfumes and detergents everywhere. Dirt and grass that people had tracked in on their shoes.

David put his nose to the ground. He sniffed down the hall in a zig-zag pattern. He smelled a raisin and the crust from a turkey and cheddar sandwich with mustard. He smelled a broken crayon and a dried-up piece of strawberry bubble gum. He smelled a pebble of purple Play-Doh.

Finally, a familiar odor tugged at his nose like he was a fish on a hook.

Bandit was close.

So was Mr. Bruce. David could smell rubber gloves and soapy mop water.

But now that David had Bandit's scent, he was unstoppable. He tracked the puppy to the door that led to the cafeteria kitchen. Even with all of the food smells—meatballs, mac and cheese, broccoli, chocolate pudding—David *knew* his puppy was on the other side of that door.

Mission accomplished.

Dogpaddle in the Dishwater

David used his snout to push open the swing-ing kitchen door. "Bandit?" he said softly.

"I found a splash place!" the puppy called.

"A what?" David followed his nose to a small room off the main kitchen. In one corner was a storage shelf. Beside that was a metal countertop with a large sink.

Bandit was already halfway up a stepladder someone had left standing open. The puppy climbed to the top step and crossed to the nearest shelf, sending stacks of paper napkins fluttering to the floor. From the shelf, he

hopped over to the countertop. "Watch this!"
He dove into the sink. Sudsy water sloshed
everywhere.

David watched Bandit dogpaddle in the
dishwater. It sure looked refreshing. He followed Bandit's path up to the sink and did a
bellyflop. His splash was even bigger than
Bandit's had been.

Bandit dipped his head and came up with
a soap bubble mustache and beard. "School is

so much fun!" he said. "I can't believe you get to come here every single day!"

"Well, it isn't always like this," David said. "Mostly we just sit and learn stuff."

"Oh. That's too bad. Hey, who was that guy who was following you?"

"That was Mr. Bruce. He's the janitor."

"What's a janitor?" Bandit swam in a circle around David, his tail going *splat splat splat* on the surface of the water. "What's a Bruce?"

"A janitor is a person whose job is to clean things. Mr. Bruce is our school janitor's name, like your name is Bandit and my name is David."

"Why were you running away from him?"

"He has a leash."

"We don't like leashes?"

"We definitely don't. If we get leashed, we won't be able to play how we want—"

"Hey! I'm starving!" The puppy climbed up onto the shiny metal counter and launched himself over the edge into the soft pile of napkins on the floor. He shook his tiny body, spraying water droplets everywhere, and then ran from the room.

"Wait for me!" David jumped down, shook himself, and followed Bandit to the pantry, where the array of smells made his mouth water and his stomach growl. As it turned out, he was hungry, too.

Bandit knocked over a basket of vegetables. Lettuce, carrots, bell peppers, and tomatoes tumbled out onto the floor. They were all shades of grayish-brown, instead of bright greens and oranges and reds. It wasn't very appetizing. Was this how colors always looked to dogs?

Maybe so, because Bandit didn't seem bothered. He tore into a head of lettuce, shaking it like it was a plush doggie toy. He bit into a bunch of carrots and spit chunks everywhere. He sniffed some tomatoes, and then he stomped on one.

"It makes a squish!" he cried. "Try it, David!"

David stepped on a tomato. *Squish*. He stepped on another, and then another, spraying juice and seeds across the tile. When the tomatoes were completely destroyed, the two dogs attacked a bin of berries. Then, they both rolled around in the muck until their coats were filthy.

"I need another bath," Bandit declared.

Back they went to the sink. After their second swim, they shook themselves dry and returned to the pantry, where they ate two whole boxes of graham crackers—including some of the cardboard packaging.

"This is perfect," David said happily. "I should've turned into a dog ages ago." If only he'd known how.

Not that he knew how he'd done it today. He guessed he was just lucky.

Don't Get Caught

While licking up graham cracker crumbs from the pantry floor, David got an amazing idea. "Follow me, Bandit," he said. "I want to show you something."

"Okay!"

The kitchen had a door that led outside. David knew this because once, during recess, he'd jumped the playground fence to sneak around the perimeter of the school. He'd been pretending to be a spy, and knowing where all the exits were was important when you were on dangerous undercover missions. He'd made it back without anyone but Owen knowing he'd been gone—which meant David was, in fact, a very good spy.

He decided to be a spy now. As he crawled out of the pantry, he slunk low, imagining a web of invisible lasers just above him. That door had to be around here somewhere. If he sniffed hard, he thought he could smell leafy trees and cut grass and fresh air.

He turned to check that his puppy was behind him and—*ack!*

"Where are you going?" he whispered.

Bandit was strutting across the kitchen floor in the opposite direction. "I smell something yummy."

"You're supposed to be following me."

"In a minute." The puppy was getting closer and closer to the cafeteria workers.

"They'll see you!" David whispered.

"So?"

"If the grown-ups catch us, the fun is over. Remember what I said about leashes?"

Bandit paused. "Oh. Right."

"Rule number one of having big ideas is: Don't get caught." David paused. "Actually, that's rule number two."

"What's rule number one?"

"Go for it!" David felt excited just *thinking* about the moment when an idea went from living inside his head to becoming real.

"Go for it," Bandit echoed. "What's 'it'?"

Before David could explain, one of the cafeteria workers called out, "Julie, can you grab some more carrots?"

"Sure." The cook nearest to Bandit and David turned.

David dove under a shelf. He waved with his paw for Bandit to do the same. But the puppy didn't hide. Instead, he pranced around in a circle so that he stayed at the woman's back, just out of sight.

"What are you doing?" David muttered.

"Going for it!" Bandit answered.

David put a paw across his eyes. "That's not what I meant!"

Any second now, Bandit would be spotted. David had to do something. He suddenly remembered how Bandit's mother had carried her puppies around in her mouth, holding them by the loose skin at the back of their neck. David's dad had called that area the "scruff." He'd told David never to pick up Bandit by his scruff. Only dogs knew how to do it safely.

David was a dog now, though.

David ran behind Julie and scooped up his puppy. The back of Bandit's neck tasted fuzzy. The fur tickled his tongue. Also, Bandit was heavier than David had expected. The puppy's feet dragged along the ground as David raced them across the length of the kitchen.

He saw a door. What if it was *the* door—the one that led outside?

It had a round metal doorknob. David had no clue how he, a dachshund, could possibly turn a knob like that. But beside the door sat a bulging garbage bag. The knot at the top looked loose. That gave David an idea.

He set Bandit down. "Stay," he ordered, and for once, the puppy listened. David used his teeth to tug at the knot until it came undone. "In." He helped Bandit into the opening. Then, he crawled into the trash himself.

Bandit yipped with glee as he burrowed deeper. "This is amazing—"

"Shh! We're not out of the woods yet!" That was an expression David's mom used. In this case, it meant they might still get caught.

"We aren't in the woods," Bandit said. "We're in the garbage."

"Hush," David said firmly.

They waited. They heard shouts as the mess they'd made in the pantry was discovered. Someone yelled, "Call Mr. Bruce!"

Finally, the top of their trash bag was cinched and re-knotted. The bag was picked up, hauled outside, and set down. David heard the sound of a heavy door slamming shut.

He used his teeth and nails to tear through the stretchy black plastic and escape into the sunshine.

What Friendship Smells Like

Bandit leaped out right behind David. The puppy was covered in vegetable peelings, yogurt drippings, and coffee grounds. He raced over to the nearest patch of lawn and began rolling around. David was equally grimy, so he did the same.

Then, he realized he had to pee. He found a shrub and tried lifting his hind leg, the way he'd seen dogs go in the past. He lost his balance immediately. He tried again . . . and toppled over again. Huh. Maybe only adult dogs could lift their legs. David didn't like feeling babyish, but he really, really had to go. He ended up copying Bandit's puppy-squat.

When they were both done, Bandit cried out, "Let's run!" He took off through the grass, David on his heels. They romped around the corner of the school building. Then Bandit pulled up short. "What . . . is . . . that?"

"That," David said proudly, "is what I wanted to show you. It's our playground."

Bandit gaped. "It's *beautiful*."

David agreed.

From his low-to-the-ground vantage point as a dachshund, the colorful metal climbing structures were steep mountains. The suspended bridge between two pieces of equipment crossed a wide canyon. The tower that housed the spiral slide rose up over the horizon like a skyscraper. The swings were hammocks and the blacktop beyond was a vast, empty desert. The fact that David couldn't see all the colors only made the playground look more alien and wondrous.

The two dogs slipped through a small opening in the fence. Then, it was like they'd been shot out of a cannon. David chased Bandit and Bandit chased David. They rolled and wrestled. They climbed and slid.

They had a make-believe battle on the suspended bridge. David was a brave knight and Bandit was a fearsome dragon. Luckily, Bandit couldn't really breathe fire. His stinky breath was bad enough.

They had a digging contest in the dirt behind the swings. When Bandit dug too deep and got stuck in his own dirt hole, David grabbed the puppy's tail with his teeth and tugged him free.

They were doing figure-eights on the black-top when David found himself slowing down. "I think I need to rest," he admitted. Trying to keep up with Bandit all morning had worn him out. "Aren't you tired?"

Bandit jogged over. "I could nap," he said. "For a few minutes."

The two of them found a quiet spot under the spiral slide. Bandit turned in a circle before settling down, so David did, too. Then, they snuggled up together.

"I'm glad you're here," Bandit said.

David smiled. "Me too."

"It's really cool that you can be either a human or a dog," Bandit said.

"Wait." David pulled away, shocked by a sudden realization. "I never told you I was a person! I never even introduced myself!" Sometimes, when David was in the middle of something big, messy, wacky, and wonderful, he forgot important details.

"In the kitchen," Bandit said, "you said your name was David."

"But . . . how did you know I was . . . *me*? Your person? Did you see me change?"

Maybe Bandit could tell David how he'd done it. Then David could learn how to do it again and again, whenever he wanted.

"I didn't see anything," the puppy said.

"So how—"

"You smelled like you."

David sniffed himself, curious. "What do I smell like?"

"My friend." Bandit let out an enormous yawn. His eyelids drooped. "You are what friendship smells like."

David's heart grew bigger inside his chest. "Thanks, buddy," he said. "You too."

Bandit began to snore.

With the puppy's rib cage rising and falling against his own furry belly, David felt drowsy and happy. The sun was high in the sky, warming the metal slide above his head. The shadows in his hiding spot were dark and cozy. The rubberized ground was soft. His belly was full. The morning had been wonderful, and the afternoon would be even more so.

After rest time, they could break into the art closet.

Or they could play ball in the gym.

Or they could . . .

David's eyelids fell closed, and he slept.

A Sinking Feeling

Someone was scratching behind David's ears. It felt really, really nice. He yawned and stretched, and then he opened his eyes.

"Owen!" he barked, jumping to his feet at the sight of his best friend. "Hi!"

"Shhhh!" Owen looked in all directions, even though they were pretty well hidden in the nook beneath the spiral slide. "Not so loud!"

David lowered his voice. "Bandit and I have been having the best time! We played in the

pantry! We swam in the sink! Mr. Bruce was chasing us, but we got away!"

"Hey, Bandit." Owen turned his attention to the smaller dachshund. "I'm really glad I found you."

"Me too!" David woofed happily. "Oh! Maybe now *you* can turn into a dog. Then you can play with us!" Something else occurred to him: "Did Mrs. Norrell call my parents yet?"

Owen didn't answer the question. Instead, he said to Bandit, "David is still out there somewhere, looking for you."

"Hold on!" David yipped. "I'm right here! It's me! David!" As his nap-fuzzies faded, he remembered that Mr. Bruce hadn't understood him—but surely best friends were different. Best friends would recognize each other in any form.

Owen patted David on the head. "It's nice that you made a new friend," he told Bandit, "but I should probably get you inside." He tucked Bandit under his t-shirt, backed out from under the slide, stood, and crossed his arms in front of his chest to hide the squirming puppy. He started walking quickly toward the door that led into the school building.

David dashed over to the thick bushes planted along the fence on this side of the playground. He ducked beneath them, staying out of sight as he trailed after Owen.

"Mrs. Norrell?" Owen called to their teacher. "I need the bathroom!"

Mrs. Norrell glanced their way. "Nate! Will you go with Owen?"

Nate trotted over. "Let's make this fast. I was examining a coleoptera by the swings, and I don't want it to get away."

"A colly-what?" Owen's eyebrows smushed together in confusion.

"A beetle," Nate said.

"Oh. Cool." Owen paused. "Can you show it to me?"

Nate raised an eyebrow. "If it's still there when we come back."

"Right. Um, you first," Owen said.

Nate went inside. Owen followed. David checked that no one was looking and tried to dart in after them, but—

"Shoo!" Owen put his foot out.

David got a sinking feeling. He tried to go around.

"Shoo!"

"What was that?" Nate asked.

"I said . . . *achoo!*" Owen pretended to sneeze.

"Bless you. What's the holdup?"

"My shoe's untied." Owen crouched, using one hand to restrain Bandit as the other fiddled with his laces. "You can't come in," he told David in a low voice.

"Why?" David whined.

"There's only supposed to be one dog at school today." Owen paused. "Well, I guess there should be zero dogs. No offense, Bandit. But anyway, you"—he booped David's nose apologetically—"don't belong here."

"I *do*! I swear—"

"I know this puppy. He lives with my best friend," Owen said. "I'm going to make sure Bandit is safe until David comes back to class. I promised David I would do whatever it takes to help." Owen looked down at Bandit. "I just hope David's parents don't decide to give you to another family, after David lost you today."

"What?" David yelped, forgetting to be quiet. "What are you talking about?"

His parents would never give Bandit away . . . would they?

Before David could woof another word, Owen stood and shut the door in his face.

The Ballad of the Closed Door

David whimpered. His eyes began to water. He felt trembly and strange.

Bandit couldn't go live with another family. He belonged with David!

How could Owen say something like that?

David scratched at the door. "Owen!" he barked, frantic. "Let me in!"

He heard a shout from the direction of the swings. "Whoa! Is that a dog?" The voice was Riley's . . . and when David turned around, he saw that she was pointing right at him.

Mrs. Norrell took a step forward, lifting a hand to shield her eyes from the sun. "Is it David's puppy?"

"I don't think that's Bandit," Madison said. "I think it's a different dachshund."

"How can you tell?" Lydia asked.

"It's bigger," Madison said.

"Yeah," agreed Riley. "And it doesn't have a mask around its eyes."

"I want to pet it!" Farrah squealed. She broke into a run.

And then everyone was running toward David, including Mrs. Norrell.

David darted for the bushes he'd hidden in earlier. *Don't get caught*. That was rule number two.

Except . . . maybe it would cheer him up to play with his friends, even if they didn't know it was him. He could definitely use some snuggles and belly-scratches right about now. He poked his head out from the bushes, ready to be adored.

"Stay back, kids." Mrs. Norrell held her arms wide. "It doesn't have a collar. It might be a stray."

"I'm not a stray!" David woofed.

"I know you all want to pet it, but it's not a good idea to pet strange dogs. Even if they seem friendly, they might bite," Mrs. Norrell said.

"I would *never*," David barked.

His teacher shook her head. "I'll find Mr. Bruce. He can catch it and call animal control."

"Aww," Farrah groaned.

"Will it get taken to the pound?" Lydia asked.

"The pound?!" David jumped backward. "I can't go to the pound! I'm a person!"

"Hopefully, this dog belongs to someone who is looking for it," Mrs. Norrell said, wringing her hands. "Let's line up and go in so I can talk to Mr. Bruce about what to do."

Just then, Owen and Nate came back out. Owen's hands were empty and his shirt hung flat on his chest. He must have left Bandit inside. But where?

"Owen, Nate, we're getting ready to head back in," their teacher said.

"We found a dog!" Farrah announced, pointing toward David. "But it's not Bandit."

Owen and Nate exchanged looks, but neither boy spoke. They just got in line with the others. Mrs. Norrell stood at the door. Her students filed inside. The door closed.

David was alone . . . for now.

Mr. Bruce would surely be here soon.

If David went to the pound, would he ever see his family again? Or Owen? Or the rest of his second-grade class?

And what would happen to Bandit? David couldn't let his parents give the puppy away.

It was time to turn back into himself.

He closed his eyes and concentrated on transforming. *I'm a human being*, he thought. *I'm David Dixon, seven-year-old kid.*

He opened his eyes. The world was still colored wrong. The ground was still too close. He still had paws and black-brown fur. He turned to check his rear end. He still had a wiry tail.

What he didn't have was his puppy. Or his best friend. Or a collar to show that he wasn't a stray. Or the slightest idea how to change from a dog into a person.

All of a sudden, it was too much. David

began to cry. He howled and yowled. He whined and wailed. This morning, he'd been a rock star. Now, he was singing the blues. This was "The Ballad of the Closed Door."

When he was all cried out, David curled his long, skinny body into a *C* and covered his face with his paws. Maybe the magic that had turned him into a dachshund would eventually just . . . wear off.

Or maybe he'd be stuck like this forever.

11

A Very Not-Helpful Bird

"**Ahem.**"

David looked up to see a small brown bird perched on the highest branch of the bush.

"Ahem," she said again, like she had a seed stuck in her throat. "Are you alright?"

"No," David said honestly.

"What's wrong?"

David was so relieved that someone other than Bandit could understand him that the story squirted out of his mouth like water from a hose. "This morning, I turned into a dog! It was a lot of fun at first, but now I don't know how to turn back! If I get sent to the pound, I'll never see my family and friends again!"

"My goodness," the bird said. She had a fancy voice, twinkly and proper.

"Also, my puppy, Bandit, is inside the school, without me. I'm supposed to take care of him. What if something happens to him? And then, what if my parents decide I'm not responsible enough to have a dog, and they give him away?"

"It sounds like you've had quite a day."

"You can say that again."

"It sounds like you've had quite a day." The bird paused. "Why did you need me to say it twice?"

"I didn't—never mind." David pushed up to a sitting position. "Do you know anything about turning people into dogs or dogs into people?"

"I'm afraid I don't."

"Have you heard about this happening to anyone else?"

"I'm afraid I haven't."

"Can you take me to someone who can help?"

"I'm afraid I can't."

"You—wait, what's your name?"

"Twyla." The bird preened. "Thank you for asking."

"Sure. Twyla, you are a very not-helpful bird."

Twyla ruffled her feathers. "There's no need to be rude!"

"Sorry," David grumbled.

"If you don't have any more questions," Twyla said stiffly, "I'll be off."

"Hold on." David tried to focus. "How come you can understand me, but Mr. Bruce and Owen and the rest of my class can't?"

"Are Mr. Bruce and Owen and the others people?"

"Yes."

"Then it's simple. Humans don't speak Animal."

"If no one understands me, how do I convince them that I'm . . . me?" David wished that humans had supercharged noses, like dogs. Bandit had recognized David's scent right away.

Twyla hopped one way on the branch. "Hm," she said. She hopped the other way. "Hm." She went back—"hm"—and forth—"hm."

Finally, David couldn't take it anymore. "What are you doing?"

"Thinking," the bird said, as if it should have been obvious.

"For that long?!"

Twyla's black eyes went wide. "Why, I'd barely begun!"

David barked in disbelief.

"I couldn't possibly give you advice without thoroughly thinking it through," Twyla said. "No, no, no. That wouldn't be responsible of me."

There was that word again: *responsible*. David groaned. He was about to talk back when the door to the school creaked open. Mr. Bruce stomped onto the playground. He was carrying an empty crate.

"How did your puppy end up at school in the first place?" Twyla asked.

"I brought him for show-and-tell," David said softly.

"Hm." Twyla fluttered down a branch. "Did you bring one of those . . . stringy things people use on dogs?"

"A leash? No. I put him in my backpack."

"Hm." The bird descended two more branches, perching right in front of David's face. "Are dogs supposed to be at school?"

"Um. Some dogs are. Like, service dogs?"

Twyla leaned in. "Is *your* dog supposed to be at school?"

David chose not to answer that.

"It seems to me," Twyla said, "that you're in a quagmire of your own making."

David frowned. "What's a quagmire?"

"A sticky situation. A precarious predicament. A mess."

"Well," David said, annoyed, "I didn't ask to turn into a dog."

"You didn't?"

David let his mind drift back to the moment it happened. "Fine, I wished it . . . but I didn't know the wish would come true!"

"Hm."

David thought he would be happy not to hear anyone say "hm" ever again.

Twyla's voice turned gentle. "All I mean to say is, if you did this, you can undo it."

"How?" David whined.

"I haven't the foggiest idea," Twyla said, and flew away.

12

Stinky-Sock Sandwiches

David scowled at Twyla, who was now a brown speck in the sky. "Thanks for nothing!" he snarled.

Halfway across the playground, Mr. Bruce froze. "I heard that," he grumbled, loud enough for David to hear. He set the crate on the blacktop and looked around, squinting.

David pressed his furry body into the dirt. He held his breath. He shut his eyes, like that would make him invisible.

And then he smelled something.

He smelled some*one*. He smelled . . . *Owen*.

Owen, he realized, smelled like pepperoni slices and mandarin oranges and colored pencils. It was a combination that shouldn't make sense, but somehow did.

The Owen scent was coming from the direction of the school. When David opened his eyes, he saw that the door was cracked a couple inches. Through the crack, he could see a sliver of his best friend's body, including one glasses-covered eye.

"Stray?" Owen whispered. "Here, doggie."

David waited for Mr. Bruce to turn his back and then peeked out of the bushes.

Owen saw him and opened the door another inch. "Come here," he murmured, beckoning with one hand.

David hesitated. Was this a trick? What if

he left his hiding place, only for Owen to shut the door in his face a second time?

No, Owen wouldn't do that. He might not recognize David as a dog, but he wasn't cruel.

"Hurry!" Owen waved his hand again.

David crept across the playground, behind the janitor's back. He felt like every hair on his body was standing on end. When he reached

Owen, his best friend scooped him up. He covered David's mouth while silently shutting the door.

When the latch clicked, David nuzzled into Owen's chest. Nuzzling, it turned out, was fantastic. He also had the strangest urge to lick Owen's face, but he made himself resist. "You came back!" he woofed quietly. "Why did you—"

"Are you sure this is a good idea?" Nate stood a few feet away, acting as lookout.

"See how friendly he is?" Owen said. "This dog has a home. He's not a stray. He's just lost." He turned to David. "You looked so sad when I left you outside. I felt bad. When I heard Mrs. Norrell and Mr. Bruce talking about the pound, I knew I had to help you."

David grinned his biggest doggie-grin.

Nate wasn't smiling. "We should get back before Mrs. Norrell gets suspicious."

Owen unzipped his bag. "Get in," he told David.

David happily obeyed. He felt even happier when he saw who else was in the backpack.

"Hi!" Bandit said. "I missed you."

"I missed you, too. Are you okay?" David sniffed Bandit all over. Everything smelled normal. That was a good sign.

"I'm great," the puppy said cheerfully. "Owen gave me his bread crusts from lunch! You picked a good best friend."

David nodded. "I sure did."

"Quiet, both of you." Owen closed the bag and hoisted it onto his back with a grunt. He started walking. David could hear Owen and Nate speaking in low voices, but he couldn't make out any words. He smelled indoor smells, like pencil shavings and floor cleaner and Elmer's glue. The air in the bag, meanwhile, had hints of old gym socks and . . . was that . . . a slice of American cheese? David sniffed deeper. Yep, his best friend's backpack definitely smelled like stinky-sock sandwiches.

For a few minutes, David let himself feel relieved. One of his problems had been solved. He was back with Bandit—and David wasn't going to let the puppy out of his sight ever again.

But he still didn't know how to transform into a human being . . . if he even could. And he was going to need to be a human being to convince his parents to let him keep Bandit, despite what had happened today.

David breathed in the backpack's stinky-sock sandwich air and sighed it back out.

"What am I gonna do?"

Out of the Bag

"Owen! Nate! There you are!"

"Sorry, Mrs. Norrell. It took us a while to find my pencil case." Owen plopped his backpack on the floor by his desk in the last row. "Thanks for letting me go look for it."

"Of course," the teacher said, "but please try to keep a closer eye on your things."

"David! Psst, David!"

David jolted in surprise. The voice wasn't Bandit's, or Owen's, or Mrs. Norrell's. In fact, it didn't belong to anyone he knew.

"David Dixon? Is that you?"

It sounded like . . . an old man. But squeakier. Like a kid pretending to be a grandpa.

David poked his head out of the zipper hole. "Who's asking?"

"Up here!" the voice called.

David saw Bagel the guinea pig waving at him from his cage on the shelf. "Bagel?" he whispered. "How did you—"

Bagel put a claw to his lips. "I'll come down." He silently unlatched his cage door and slipped out, closing it behind him. Then he disappeared from view, only to show up a minute later on the floor behind Owen's desk, out of sight of the rest of the class. "That's better," the guinea pig said. "Now we can talk—"

"Hello!" Bandit's head popped up. "Who are you?"

"I'm Bagel, the class pet."

"I'm Bandit!" the puppy said. "Hey, we're both pets!"

The guinea pig chuckled. "That's true. Now, David—"

"What do you do in that cage all day?" Bandit asked. "Do you have any toys?"

"Not now, buddy." David turned to Bagel. "How do you know I'm David Dixon?"

"I've seen dozens of Mrs. Norrell's students transform," Bagel said. "You left the room this morning and never came back, and nobody seemed terribly worried."

"No one was worried about me?" David frowned, feeling a little hurt.

"That's how it works," Bagel said kindly. "While you're off on your animal adventure, things get a little . . . foggy for everyone else." He nodded up at Owen. "When I saw your friend's backpack moving, well, I took an educated guess."

"Oh."

The guinea pig cocked his head. "So, David, how's your day been?"

"Epic!" Bandit blurted. "We're having so much—"

"Fun," David finished, wishing his puppy wouldn't speak for him.

Above them, Owen fake-coughed and nudged the backpack with his heel.

Bagel raised a tiny, hairy eyebrow. "The whole day has been fun?"

"Yes!" Bandit yipped.

David thought about how it had felt to hear Owen wonder if Bandit would be given away. He thought about feeling alone and scared when he realized he might get taken to the pound. He thought about crying as he howled "The Ballad of the Closed Door."

"Not everything was fun," he whispered.

"Are you ready to change back into yourself?" Bagel asked.

"Yes! But . . ." David couldn't resist asking, "Can I turn into a dog again sometime?"

"Sorry, this is a one-time deal," Bagel said. "Every kid in this class will get a single chance to transform—if you don't spoil the surprise." He leaned in close, stern-faced. "No spilling the secret! Got it?"

David looked up at his best friend. "I can't even tell Owen?"

"Not if you want him to have his turn with the magic."

"Okay. I won't tell." David raised a paw like he was solemnly swearing.

"Good. So, how it works is—"

"What's that stuff over there?" Bandit interrupted. "Is it for making art? Let's make art!"

"Bandit, I'm trying to *listen*," David said.

"Or we could find the janitor's closet," Bandit went on. "I bet Mr. Bruce has a ton of stuff to play with. Like toilet paper!"

"No! Not Mr. Bruce!" David yelped.

Above them, Owen fake-coughed again.

"Are you okay, Owen?" Mrs. Norrell asked.

"Dry throat," Owen said. "Can I visit the water fountain?"

Before Mrs. Norrell could answer, Bandit sprang out of Owen's bag. "Freedom!"

David howled in frustration. "Nooooo!"

"Owwwww!" Owen pretended to stub his toe. But it was too late for tricks. Bandit was running for the door.

The puppy was David's responsibility.

He had no choice but to leap out of the bag after him.

14

The Problem with Puppies

"Bandit! Come back here!" David barked.

"Look! It's Bandit!" Hector shouted as the puppy raced past his desk.

"And the other dog!" Riley yelled as David zipped by. "The one from outside!"

"Owen had them!" Farrah screeched. "They were in his backpack!"

"Owen!" Mrs. Norrell gasped. "Is this true?"

"I—um—" Owen stammered. ". . . yes?"

Mrs. Norrell threw open the classroom door. "Mr. Bruce!" she called.

Bandit darted between her legs. Mrs. Norrell lunged for him, tripped over her feet, and ended up on the floor. David jumped over her ankles. His teacher grabbed at him, but only managed to brush his tail with her fingertips.

"Stop!" David called to Bandit, following him down the long hallway. "You need to stick with me from now on!"

"I have an idea!" the puppy shouted back.

The problem with puppies, David realized suddenly, was that they could be incredibly fun . . . but also incredibly exasperating. They didn't stay put. They didn't listen. They just chased whatever idea popped into their heads—and then *you* had to chase *them*.

"Now's not the time for ideas!" David yelled.

"You said 'go for it' was rule number one!"

"I did say that, but sometimes, you *shouldn't* go for it! Sometimes, you just have to sit still and do as you're told!"

Whoa.

Had those words really come out of David's mouth? Had he transformed into his mother, or his father, or his teacher, or even Twyla, the very not-helpful bird? He checked behind him for his tail. It was still there, which meant he was still David the dachshund.

Bandit began to sing. "I'm neeeever going to stop ruuuuunning!" he howled. "Ruuuuunning is my faaaaavorite! Ah-wooooo!"

The two dogs turned a corner. David was
catching up.

Then Bandit's singing was replaced by a
yelp of alarm. The puppy skidded sideways.
He slammed into the wall. His little body
slumped.

"Bandit!" David shouted. What had just
happened?

A second later, he found out.

"Aaiiiieeeee!" His feet hit a patch of slick,

wet tile. David slipped and scrambled and spun, ending up splayed on his belly.

Mr. Bruce stepped out from the closest classroom. "Gotcha," he said, placing a bright yellow "Caution: Wet Floor" sign in the middle of the hallway.

In his other hand, he held that crate again. Its metal cage door swung open with an ominous squeak.

Across the hall, Bandit was whimpering. "Ow, ow, ow, ow," he whined.

"What's wrong?" David began to crawl toward him. "Where does it hurt?"

"My paw! I twisted it! Ow, ow, ow!"

The puppy's mournful cries made David's heart feel like it was twisted, too. "I'm coming, buddy," he said.

David glanced back to see Mr. Bruce step onto the section of floor that was slippery and wet. The janitor's feet immediately went out from under him. He landed on his backside with a roar of frustration.

He wouldn't be down for long.

"David, it hurts!" Bandit whimpered.

"I know," David said. "I'm so sorry."

David reached Bandit and grabbed him by the scruff of the neck, like he had in the kitchen earlier. He managed to make it to the dry floor with the puppy before Mr. Bruce was upright again. Then he took off.

It was time to be responsible—and David thought he finally understood what that meant.

First, he would get Bandit to Mrs. Norrell. The teacher would call his parents. Then— once he was sure Bandit was going to be taken care of—David would figure out how to turn back into himself.

David turned the corner into the long hallway that led to his second-grade classroom. He crossed over the spot where he'd wished to be a dog, and then had magically become one.

"What's that smell?" Bandit asked, sniffing the air.

It was . . . lemon-lime shampoo squirted over a stinky wet dog.

"Ooh, what's that sound?" The puppy's ears lifted.

Wind chimes. A popping balloon.

"Brrrr!" Bandit shivered as a cold breeze rushed over them both.

David kept running. But something felt different.

He was . . . taller.

He looked down. He was jogging on two very human legs. He held his puppy tight in two very human arms. He had pale skin rather than black-brown fur. Also, he wore clothes. He hadn't thought of it before, but as a dachshund, he'd been naked. Ha!

Once he started laughing, he couldn't stop.

Big, Messy, Wacky, and Wonderful

David was still snickering when he walked into his classroom. He stopped when he saw Mrs. Norrell. She had a hand pressed to her forehead, and one eye was squinting.

"David," she said faintly. "You're back."

"I am. And I found Bandit. He hurt his paw. We need to call my parents."

Mrs. Norrell nodded. "Let me get someone to watch the class while you and I go to

Mr. Angelo's office." The teacher stepped out into the hall.

"Took you long enough," Riley said to David.

"Owen found Bandit first!" Farrah pointed out.

David smiled at his best friend. "I know. Thanks for watching out for us, Owen."

"Us?" Tally's voice rang out sharply. It was surprising to hear her speak so loudly. She wasn't as shy as she'd been on the first day of school, but she still didn't love when everyone looked at her. "Um," she said, blushing a little, "did you mean, he watched out for Bandit?"

"Yes," David said quickly. "That's what I meant."

Tally stared at him. Her gaze was so sharp, it was like she was trying to see through him. Did he have something on his face? He checked and didn't feel anything.

"Okay," Mrs. Norrell said, reentering the room with one of the kindergarten teachers. "Mr. DeLeon is going to stay with you until David and I come back. Behave yourselves!" She turned to David. "Shall we?"

"I guess so."

David tucked Bandit underneath his shirt and crossed his arms over his chest, like Owen had during recess. The puppy was not getting away from him again. Not that Bandit could run very far with a twisted paw.

This was the part of an adventure that was sometimes not so great.

Sometimes, there were consequences. When David had splatter-painted the garage door, his parents had made him pay to have it repainted using his allowance. So, he hadn't been able to buy the toy robot he'd been saving up for. Meanwhile, thanks to their blood vessel caper at the science museum last year, David and Owen now had to bring parents with them on field trips. One-on-one supervision made the outings a lot less fun.

Listening to Bandit whimper felt worse than not getting a robot. It definitely felt worse than having a parent come along on a field trip.

David hated that his puppy was in pain. He hated even more that it was his fault.

"I'm sorry I brought Bandit to school," he told Mrs. Norrell. "I thought it was the best idea ever, but I know now that it wasn't."

"Sometimes," his teacher said, "ideas seem good until you stop to think about them."

"I—" David's breath hitched. "I don't want my parents to decide I can't be trusted with a puppy. I don't want them to give Bandit away."

"Well, let's talk about what you learned today," Mrs. Norrell said. "What was your plan when you brought Bandit to school?"

"I would show him off . . ."

"And then what? He would sit quietly under your desk?"

David snorted. "Bandit would never do that."

"Ah."

"I guess I . . . didn't look that far ahead."

"We can work on that together this year, if you'd like." Mrs. Norrell paused. "Your parents might like to hear that you're working on that with me."

David remembered what Twyla had said about thoroughly thinking things through. Maybe that very not-helpful bird had been onto something. Hm.

Not that David was done having big ideas. No way! Having big ideas was as much a part of David as his dark brown hair and the jellyfish-shaped freckle behind his right knee. But maybe, with his teacher's guidance, he'd end up in fewer quagmires.

"Okay," he said, and Mrs. Norrell looked pleased.

They entered the main office. Mrs. Norrell went to speak to the principal. Mrs. Philippidis smiled at David from her desk. He couldn't help sniffing the air to see if he could catch her signature sugar-cookie-and-pine-cone scent. Sadly, he was back to having a human nose, and it just wasn't sharp enough.

While Mrs. Norrell called his parents, David sat and waited. His mind did what it usually did when he was asked to sit and wait. He got ideas.

Big, messy, wacky, wonderful ideas.

The small room that held the enormous copy machine was empty. What if David copied something silly and posted the pictures all over the school? Or . . . what if he took the paper, and made a million paper airplanes, and went up to the roof and threw them off, one by one, to see which design flew the farthest—

He looked down at his puppy, now snoring softly inside his shirt.

Maybe, he thought, today had been big, messy, wacky, and wonderful enough.

Ten Fun Facts about Dachshunds

 Dachshund is a German word made up of two parts: *dachs*, meaning "badger," and *hund*, meaning "dog." First bred in Germany as hunting dogs, dachshunds have long, low-to-the-ground bodies that are ideal for digging into a badger's underground den. That distinctive sausage shape is also why dachshunds are known as "wiener dogs."

Dachshunds come in two sizes: standard and miniature. Standard dachshunds weigh 16 to 32 pounds, while miniature dachshunds weigh up to 11 pounds. (Dachshunds between 11 and 16 pounds are unofficially known as "tweenies.") David turns into a standard dachshund, like his puppy, Bandit. At eight weeks old, Bandit weighs about 5 pounds. David is about 10 pounds, which is closer to the size of a six-month-old puppy.

3 Is it true that one year in a dog's life equals seven human years? Not exactly. Dogs age much more quickly at the beginning of their lives, so a one-year-old dog is more like a fifteen-year-old human. The rate of aging slows down as dogs reach middle age. Additionally, small dogs tend to live longer than large ones, with dachshunds usually living twelve to sixteen years.

4 David's family adopts Bandit when he's eight weeks old. That's the age many veterinarians and breeders feel is safe for puppies to be separated from their mothers, although some experts prefer to wait until twelve weeks.

It's a myth that dogs see in black and white. Dogs do see some colors: blues and yellows, but not reds, oranges, or greens. In addition to experiencing a smaller range of colors, dogs generally have worse daytime vision than people; this is why David's eyesight is a little fuzzy during his time as a dachshund. However, dogs see *much* better than humans in low light.

 David isn't wrong to imagine that as a dog, he has a supercharged nose. A dog's sense of smell can be 10,000 to 100,000 times stronger than a human's, and the area of a dog's brain that analyzes odors is about forty times larger. Thanks to their background as hunting dogs, dachshunds have some of the best noses out there, with 125 million scent receptors. (A human has 5 or 6 million, while the bloodhound—the dog breed with the most powerful sense of smell—has 300 million!)

 Not only can dogs that were bred to hunt distinguish individual scents from one another, they can also tell how fresh a scent is. This helps them move in the correct direction toward their target. Dachshunds and other hounds will often be single-minded in pursuit of a scent—just like David is when tracking his lost puppy.

8 Dachshunds are known for being energetic, playful, intelligent, and stubborn. That last trait helps when they're chasing down a scent . . . but it can make training them a challenge.

9 Though they're small dogs, dachshunds can have a big bark! For hunting dogs, that bark alerts humans that the prey has been found. Pet dachshunds will bark when they're feeling excited, anxious, hungry, bored, territorial, or in need of some extra attention.

10 Dachshunds are energetic dogs that need exercise and activity. In addition to daily walks, they enjoy playing, digging, and even swimming (but they should always wear a life jacket in the water). Physical and mental stimulation keep dachshunds happy, healthy, and out of trouble.

Acknowledgments

Thanks to:

- My editor, Erica Finkel, whose insightful notes helped David become more himself.
- My agent, Alyssa Eisner Henkin, who always has my back.
- Ariel Landy and Okan Bülbül, whose illustrations bring the characters to life.
- The Amulet team: editorial director Maggie Lehrman; associate editor Emily Daluga; associate managing editor Megan Carlson; production associate Jenn Jimenez; designer Jade Rector and associate art director Deena Fleming; publicist Mary Marolla; and publisher Andrew Smith.
- Every friend and family member who's listened to my big, messy, wacky, and wonderful ideas (and chimed in with their own).
- Justin and Evie—my favorites, forever.

About the Author

Kathryn Holmes always dreamed of telling stories for a living. These days, she writes books for kids and teens. Originally from Maryville, Tennessee, she went to Goucher College in Baltimore, Maryland, where she majored in dance and English literature. She later received her MFA in Writing for Children from The New School in New York City. Kathryn now lives in Brooklyn, New York, with her husband and daughter. You can find her online at kathrynholmes.com.

Also Available

CLASS CRITTERS

Tally Tuttle Turns into a Turtle

Kathryn Holmes